The Invasion of the Shag Carpet Creature

Other Horace Splattly Books:

Horace Splattly: The Cupcaked Crusader

Horace Splattly, The Cupcaked Crusader:
When Second Graders Attack

Horace Splattly, The Cupcaked Crusader:
The Terror of the Pink Dodo Balloons

Horace Splattly, The Cupcaked Crusader:
To Catch a Clownosaurus

Horace Splattly

THE CUPCAKED CRUSADER

The Invasion of the Shag Carpet Creature

by **Lawrence David**

illustrated by **Barry Gott**

Dutton Children's Books · New York

For Princess Betsy "Smellen" David, my only sister,
who, when she was four, used to cry when Mom
tried to make her wear a dress, because then she
couldn't be like her four older brothers

—L.D.

Text copyright © 2004 by Lawrence David
Illustrations copyright © 2004 by Barry Gott

CIP DATA IS AVAILABLE
ISBN 0-525-47235-5

Published simultaneously by Dutton Children's Books and Puffin Books,
divisions of Penguin Young Readers Group
345 Hudson Street, New York, New York 10014
www.penguin.com

Designed by Tony Sahara
Printed in USA

First Edition

1   3   5   7   9   10   8   6   4   2

Contents

Sara Willow's Wild Ride

"I'll put the quarter in!" Sara Willow told her little brother. "You get in the car."

"Okay, sis," Willy Willow told his older sister. He climbed up and sat in the miniature car outside the Craft Barn. The car was attached to a pole in a machine. Sara put a coin in the slot then got in next to her brother. The car rocked back and forth. Sara and Willy laughed.

Horace sat in the food court at the Blootinville Mall and watched them. He was eating celernip curly fries covered in wild

Blootinberry sauce. The rest of his family were trying on fake animal ears at the Ear Emporium. The Splattlys were going to the first ever Splattly and Blattly family reunion tomorrow, and Horace's sister had the idea that the whole family should wear matching fake animal ears to the event.

His mom and dad liked the idea. Horace thought it was the stupidest idea he'd ever heard. After all, each of them already had two *real* human ears. Why did they need matching fake animal ears?

"Oh my!" Sara Willow cried. "It's going too fast!"

The miniature car jerked back and forth, and the pole rose higher in the air. Horace watched as Sara Willow's hair bounced around her head. He thought she was the most beautiful girl he'd ever seen in his life. In fact, he thought she was even more beautiful than celernip curly fries with wild Blootinberry sauce. She wore her hair in a different style every day. Today, it was in the shape of an octopus. There was one large ball of hair on top and eight long octopus arms swinging around her face with large rubber suction cups attached to the ends.

The miniature car rocked faster and faster, lurching forward, backward, and side to side. Sara and Willy were moving so fast, they were just a blur.

"Make it stop!" Sara screamed. Two of her tentacles swung into her eyes and stuck there. "I can't see!"

"My fingernails feel like they're flying off!" Willy cried.

The car began spinning in circles like a top.

People gathered around the ride.

"Someone help them!"

"It's gone wild!" Mr. Willow screamed. "Someone unplug it!"

But the ride was jerking around so fast that no one could get close enough to unplug it. If someone didn't stop it soon, the Willow kids would be blended like a milk shake.

Horace reached into his coat pocket and

pulled out half a cupcake. It had yellow icing and cake that looked as bright as the neon sign hanging over the Ear Emporium.

Ten-year-old Horace Splattly popped the piece of cupcake into his mouth. This looked like a job for the Cupcaked Crusader.

• • •

The Cupcaked Crusader was his sister's idea. Eight-year-old Melody Splattly was a homemaker-scientist-decorator-inventor-genius. She invented purple fingernail polish that could also fill cavities. She invented boots with toes that spit salt to melt snow wherever you walked. And she invented the cupcakes Horace ate that gave him superpowers so he could become the Cupcaked Crusader.

Melody usually gave Horace the cupcakes so he could help her do things. Once, she gave him a cupcake that turned one of his hands into a towel, his other hand into a soap bottle, and made his forehead into a squeegee. She swung

Horace from a rope off the roof of their house and made him soap, clean, and dry all the windows. She told him that if he didn't do it, she'd beat him up. Since Horace was the shortest kid in all of Blootinville Elementary but for the kindergartners and six of the first graders, and since Melody was over a foot taller than her brother, she *really could* beat her older brother up if she wanted to.

Last night, she had baked the bright yellow cupcake because she wanted Horace to spy on her archenemy, Penny Honey. Melody hated Penny because her family was rich. Melody had wanted Horace to see what Penny was wearing to school today so she could wear something even prettier. She had given Horace the cupcake then told him to wear the Cupcaked Crusader costume she had made. "If someone spots you, just say you're protecting the neighborhood," Melody had told him, giving him a slap on the back. "You're a superhero! That's what superheroes do."

Horace fell forward onto his sister's bed. "I'm only a superhero when you let me be a superhero," he told his sister. "The powers wear off, and then I'm just the brother you order around. What good is it being a superhero if no one knows?"

"Stop whining," Melody had said. "You're lucky I'm smart enough to make the cupcakes that make you a superhero for even a little while."

Melody didn't want anyone to know Horace was really the Cupcaked Crusader, because if their parents found out, they'd take away all the Lily Deaver bakeware and science equipment she used to make her inventions.

Horace had put on the costume, eaten the cupcake, and gotten the special powers. Then he went over to Penny Honey's house and spied in her bedroom window to find out what the eight-year-old girl was wearing to school so his sister could wear something prettier this morning.

And Melody did. All day long, Horace's sister strutted the hallways in a lavender Lily Deaver feathered gown and hat while Penny Honey sulked in her fake zebra-print skirt and matching blouse.

What Melody didn't know was that her brother had eaten only half of the cupcake and had pocketed the other half to save for when *he* wanted to be a superhero.

• • •

The out-of-control car ride bounced, jostled, and careened, flinging Sara's and Willy's arms in every direction as if they were rag dolls. People had to duck to keep from getting slapped across the face with Sara's octopus-arm hair.

Horace swallowed the second half of the cupcake and ducked behind the mall map in the corner of the food court. He reached into his inside jacket pocket and pulled out his Cupcaked Crusader costume. He took the purple taffeta outfit with him almost everywhere he went. After all, a superhero never knew when he might suddenly have to save a pretty girl from a miniature car ride at a shopping mall.

And it was a good thing he did. Sara Willow always seemed to get herself into trouble, and he always had to keep saving her.

Horace slipped the costume on over his clothes just as the itching started at the top of his head. Horace scratched his fingernails across his scalp. The itching spread down his arms. Horace crossed his arms and scratched his elbows. It was like mosquitoes had bitten every inch of his body. The itching traveled over his stomach, down the back of his legs, and around his ankles to his toes.

Finally, the itching stopped. He stepped out from behind the mall map. The car ride had gone completely berserk, like a bull seeing red. Smoke poured out of the car, and it bucked so fast that Horace couldn't see Sara or her brother. He could only hear their screaming.

"Oh-me-oh-me-oh-my!" Sara screamed. "What's going on?"

"I think my nose is sliding off my face!" Willy cried.

Horace leapt atop a table and struck a pose, placing his fists on his hips. "Don't worry, folks!" he announced. "The Cupcaked Crusader is here to save the day!"

The people cheered. Everyone in Blootinville knew the Cupcaked Crusader saved people.

Horace jerked his arms from side to side, swiveling his hips as if he were inside a blender.

People stared.

Mrs. Snugget waved a hand at Horace. "Mr.

Cupcaked Crusader? Aren't you supposed to be saving the Willows?"

Mr. Willow ran over to the Cupcaked Crusader. "Stop dancing like a rock star and save my babies!" he screamed.

Horace felt like a wind-up toy. The harder he swung his hips, the stronger he could feel the power build inside him.

Just when it looked as if the car ride would explode off the pole, Horace lifted his arms over his head. His body immediately began spinning like a top, twisting faster and faster until the Cupcaked Crusader twirled across the floor like a thirty-inch top.

Chapter
2

HERO TAKES A SPIN

Horace whipped across the mall floor, aiming for the miniature car. He spun inside the cloud of smoke surrounding the ride and saw the Willows in the wild, bucking car.

"Don't worry, the Cupcaked Crusader is here," Horace said in his Cupcaked Crusader voice.

He dipped both his arms down, wrapped one around Sara, one around her brother, and pulled them free of the car. He shot out of the smoke cloud and twisted across the floor, coming to a stop by the Pretzel-Mania stand. He set both kids down gently. Sara and Willy were so dizzy that they toppled to the ground. Sara pulled her octopus arm suction cups out of her eyes so she could see again.

The only problem was that Horace's powers weren't used up yet. He couldn't stop himself from spinning. He blasted straight across the mall through the crowd of people.

"The Cupcaked Crusader's out of control!" a woman shouted.

"He's tornado-crazy!" a man yelled, darting behind the counter at Meat Loaf Heaven.

Horace crashed through the Radical Puppet Palace, the Hobo-Robot Boutique, and the Fish Stick Jewelry Shack. Clothes, necklaces, and food swirled around him in a storm. A moment later, the powers ran out, and he dropped to the floor in a heap of fried-fish earrings, robot parts, and sock puppets.

Sara and Willy ran to him.

"You're my stinky-fish hero!" Sara cried, giving Horace a hug while holding her nose.

Horace was glad to get a hug from Sara, but he had to clutch his head to keep it from feeling as if it would fall off. His eyes couldn't stop rolling in their sockets. "Uh, thank you, miss. Uh, it's all in a day's work for a superhero," he said.

Mr. Willow shook Horace's hand. "Thanks for saving my kids," he said. Then he led his kids away, and the crowd went back to shopping.

The owner of the jewelry store scolded the superhero. "Try to control your powers better next time," he said. "Fish-stick earrings don't grow on trees."

"Sorry, sir. Sometimes I'm more powerful than I think," Horace said. He looked up and spotted his parents and sister stepping out of the Ear Emporium.

"Where'd Horace wander off to?" Mrs. Splatly asked. "He said he'd be waiting by the food court."

Horace dashed behind the mall map, pulled off his Cupcaked Crusader costume, and rushed over to where he'd been sitting before he saved Sara and Willy. He stood up. "Hey, Mom and Dad, I'm right here!" he called.

Melody laughed. "Horace is so little, we couldn't see him behind the trash can." She gave her brother a pat on the head. "You're even smaller than your pile of curly fries. I better eat some so we don't get confused and lose you in them." She took a fistful of fries and stuffed them in her mouth.

Horace frowned. He'd just saved the prettiest girl in the world from a mad car ride, yet only seconds later his sister was making fun of him! Horace picked up his fries and sauce and tossed them in the trash. "Sometimes a superhero just can't win," he muttered to himself.

• • •

The Splattlys walked through the parking lot. Melody waved the bag from the Ear Emporium in her brother's face. "Wait until you see the ears we got. We bought matching sets. I didn't want to get you any, but mom and dad said that since you're a part of the family, you should have some, too," Melody said.

Horace looked at the paper bag. It seemed awfully big to be holding four sets of animal ears. What animal had such giant ears that Melody would need to carry them in a giant bag? "What kind of ears are they?" Horace asked. "Elephant ears?"

Melody held the bag closed. "You didn't come into the store, so you don't get to see," she said.

Horace was about to complain to his mom and dad, but then he stepped on something that caught his attention. "Hey, look at this," he said. He was standing on a small patch of bright blue shag carpeting. It had a weird, puddle shape, and the blue strands of shag looked as if they were trying to grow around his sneakers.

The Splattlys looked at Horace standing on the shag carpet in the middle of the parking lot.

"Someone must have dropped it after visiting your cousin Crarpet Splattly's rug store," Mrs. Splattly said.

Horace looked across the mall to the Shag

Shack. A big sign in front of the store read GET THE RUG THAT'S ALSO A PET!

Dr. Splattly nodded. "Crarpet must have made it to get people excited about blue shag rugs. You can ask him about it when we see him at the reunion."

Horace stepped off the patch of rug and looked at it again. It looked even bigger than it had been only a few seconds ago. "Can I get a pet rug?" Horace asked.

Mrs. Splattly shook her head. "You know Melody and I are allergic to pets," she told him. "All the Blattly women are."

"Hurry along, Horace," Dr. Splattly told his son. "We have to pack for the reunion tomorrow."

Horace shrugged at the shag carpet, turned around, and ran to catch up with his family.

Chapter 3

THE GREAT SPLATTLY-BLATTLY
FEUD OF 1972

"**P**ut them on!" Melody hollered.

"I'll put them on when I get there. I don't have to wear them in the car," Horace told her.

"Mom, Horace won't put his ears on! He put them away in his knapsack," Melody said, leaning over the front seat.

"He doesn't have to wear them now if he doesn't want to," Mrs. Splattly said.

"But you will wear them when we get to the reunion," Dr. Splattly told his son. "We didn't buy you such nice fake animal ears so that they'd go to waste."

The Splattly family rode along the highway that Saturday morning, excited to get to the reunion and see the Splattly and Blattly families.

"You have to wear the ears when we meet Cousin Sugar," Melody told her brother. "I'm sharing a room with her, so I want us all to make a good first impression." She leaned over the front seat. "I don't think Horace likes the ears we picked out. I think he's going to ruin my time with Sugar."

"Don't you like the ears, Horace?" Mrs. Splattly asked.

Horace looked at the heads of his sister, his mom, and his dad. The minute they got in the car, they had put their ears on.

They weren't elephant ears. Elephant ears would have been great compared to what these were.

These were giant, rubber, purple Blat bat ears! They were a foot tall and had lots of little hairs growing out of them! They were the ugliest ears Horace had ever seen in his life. Melody picked them out because Blat bats were the Blattly family's favorite animals.

Horace leaned forward to the front seat. "I do like the ears," he said. "I just think it's too early in the morning to wear bat ears."

"Well, I hope you kids have a great time at the reunion. This is the first time the Splattly and Blattly families have gotten together since our wedding," Mrs. Splattly said. "Before your dad and I got married, our families hated one another."

"They did?" Horace asked.

Dr. Splattly laughed. "Way back when your mom and I were kids in second grade, your mom and my sister were best, best friends. Then my sister got a pet rabbit named Sniffles."

Mrs. Splattly frowned at Dr. Splattly. "Let's not talk about Sniffles in front of the children, Hinkle," she said. "I'll be nice to your sister at the reunion, but I don't want the rabbit mentioned."

Horace rested his chin on the back of the

front seat. "What's the matter with Sniffles?"

Horace's dad grinned. "Well, Aunt Myrtle loved Sniffles and took him everywhere," he said. "The problem was that your mom was allergic to Sniffles, so she couldn't play with Aunt Myrtle anymore because Sniffles was there. Anytime your mom got near Sniffles, she'd sneeze and her eyes would get itchy and teary. Your mom told Myrtle she had to get rid of Sniffles or she couldn't be her friend anymore."

"And Myrtle chose Sniffles over me," Mrs. Splattly said. She folded her arms across her chest and stuck out her bottom lip. "I'll never forgive her for that."

Dr. Splattly laughed again. "That's when the families started feuding. My family was mad at your mother, and the Blattlys were mad at Myrtle. When your mom and I fell in love, our families finally forgave one another. All except for your mom and Myrtle," he explained. "They still don't get along."

Mrs. Splattly wagged her finger at Horace's

dad. "I wish you hadn't brought Sniffles up. I get angry just thinking about how your sister liked that rabbit more than me!"

Horace sat back in his seat. He'd never seen his mom so mad about anything before. Could grown-ups really be so angry about something that happened such a long time ago?

He stared out the window as the sun began to rise over Blootinville. Melody had made cupcakes that gave him powers to fly, twist, grow knitting-needle fingers, and lots of other things, but could she make a cupcake that would give him the power to stop his mom from being angry with Aunt Myrtle? He turned to ask his sister if she knew how to make one like that, when something out the window caught his eye. "Yowee-zowee-zooks! Stop!" he called.

Dr. Splatly slammed on the brakes. "What's wrong? What happened?"

"What is it, Horace?" Mrs. Splattly asked.

Horace pointed to the Blootinville Mall. It was completely covered by a giant, bright blue

shag carpet. The carpet covered the sides and roof of the mall and the entire parking lot. It had grown over lampposts, traffic signs, windows, and cars that had been left in the parking lot overnight.

"What in heaven's name is that about?" Mrs. Splattly asked. She reached into her pocketbook, took out her cell phone, and dialed. "I'll see if the newspaper knows anything about it." She was the publisher of the *Blootinville Banner* and could ask her reporters to find out what was happening.

Melody pointed out her window. "Look down the street at the Tippy-Toe Dance Hall," she said.

The Splattlys leaned out their car windows, all wearing their bat ears except for Horace. They looked at the dance hall. It was also covered in bright blue shag carpet and so was the Nip & Tuck Plastic Surgery Center.

Horace poked his dad on the shoulder. "What do you think is going on?" he asked.

Mrs. Splattly spoke into the phone. "Gus,

have you heard anything about a blue shag carpet over at the mall?" she asked.

Horace remembered the carpet from the day before and the sign outside cousin Crarpet's Shag Shack. Was this one of his pets?

Dr. Splattly looked from the mall to the dance hall to the plastic surgery center. "I think it's just one of Crarpet's ads to make everyone want blue shag carpet pets."

Mrs. Splattly dropped her cell phone back in her bag. "No one at the paper knows a thing about it, but Gus said he'd call if they heard any news."

Horace sat back in his seat as Dr. Splattly drove down the road to the family reunion. Was something wrong? Was his dad right and it was only an ad for the Shag Shack? Horace turned around and looked out the back window, watching as the blue shag carpet grew up and over the statue of Mayor Blootin in the town center.

This didn't look like any carpet ad Horace had ever seen before.

Chapter 4

THE 150-FOOT-TALL STALAGMITE

The Splattlys drove over Rumbly Mountain, through the Valley of Whittling Squirrels, and arrived at the far side of Blootinville by Celernip Bay. The richest people in town like the Blootins and the Honeys had vacation homes right on the beach. Other families like the Splattlys stayed in motels or hotels and enjoyed swimming in the summer or walking on the beach and collecting seashells in the fall.

Dr. Splattly pulled the car into a parking

space. Hotel Stalagmite was 150 feet high. At the bottom it was big and wide, but as it got higher and higher, it got thinner and thinner until there was only one room at the very top.

Dr. and Mrs. Splattly got out of the car and went around back to the trunk. "This is where your dad and I stayed after we got married," Mrs. Splattly told the kids. She leaned over and gave their dad a kiss. "We stayed in the honeymoon suite. It was very romantic."

Dr. Splattly smiled at Melody and Horace. "Maybe when you both grow up and get married, you can stay here for your honeymoons. Wouldn't that be nice?"

Melody put her hands on her hips. "I don't plan on dating or getting married," she told her parents. "I'll be far too busy running the World-Famous Melody Splattly Invention Factory, and Horace will be too busy being my secretary to meet anyone who'd want to marry him. He's lucky I'm such a nice sister that I'll give him a job." She gave her brother a slap on the back and leaned in close to his ear and whispered, "Now go put on your Blat bat ears and fetch my suitcase, or I'll tell all the Splattlys and Blattlys about the time when Mrs. Tutwiddle made you the baby in the school play and you had to go onstage wearing a diaper."

Horace grimaced and stuck his Blat ears atop his head. A sea breeze blew, flapping the ears in front of his eyes. "Why did she get to grow up big and smart? Aren't older brothers supposed to be bigger and smarter?" Horace frowned and picked up Melody's and his suitcases.

"My, what a gentleman you are, Horace," Dr. Splattly said.

"Those ears look great on you," Mrs. Splattly said, giving her ears a pull. "Are mine on straight?"

Dr. Splattly kissed his wife's cheek. "You look spectacularly Blat batty."

The Splattlys entered the hotel lobby. A big banner hung across the ceiling: THE HOTEL STA-

"I'll go get the room keys," Melody said, skipping to the front desk.

Horace's mom ran over and gave Granny Splattly a hug. Horace's dad rushed over and gave Nana Blattly a kiss. All across the lobby Splattlys and Blattlys said hello to one another. Splattly men shook hands with Blattly men. Splattly women kissed the cheeks of Blattly women. Horace found it hard to imagine that there had ever been a time when the two families hadn't gotten along.

"Oh, here's my itty-witty Horace!" Nana Blattly yelled, picking Horace up and hugging him to her body. "And I love the Blat bat ears! What fun!" Nana Blattly was a big, tall lady. Horace thought she looked like a refrigerator with bright red hair.

Horace kissed her cheek. "Hey, Nana. I think you better put me down before you crush me like a peanut shell," he said.

As soon as she put him down, Granny Splattly came over and picked him up. She had thin sticklike legs and arms, but a large round body and head. Horace thought she looked like a snowlady. "Don't you ever grow?" she asked, poking Horace with a thin finger. "I hope you're not shrinking." She put the forefinger of her left hand on her chin and the forefinger of her right hand in her ear and twisted it in a circle, getting into her thinking pose. "Hmmm . . . I'm going to make sure you eat lots and lots of spicy blab-

bage soup this weekend. That'll help you grow."

Horace kissed her cheek. "Don't worry, Granny, I'm not shrinking. I promise I don't need blabbage soup."

A tall woman with a young girl came over and stood by Horace. "Well, aren't you simply adorable," she said, raising her eyebrows. The woman looked a lot like Horace's dad, only prettier and with longer hair. She gave Horace a peck on the forehead. "I'm your Auntie Myrtle," she said.

Mrs. Splattly stepped forward and put her

hands on Horace's shoulders. "Hello, Myrtle," she said in an icy voice. "How are things hopping?"

Myrtle smirked at Horace's mother. "Hello, Mari," she said. "Been sniffling much today?"

Mrs. Splattly's face turned red with anger. Dr. Splattly stepped between his wife and sister. "Why don't we introduce the kids?" he suggested.

Aunt Myrtle nodded. "Good idea, Hinkle." She placed her hands on the shoulders of the girl in front of Horace. "This is Sugar," Aunt Myrtle said. "She's the same age as your sister."

The little girl had long blonde hair in two pigtails. She kind of looked like Little Bo-Peep, only instead of a sheep, she held a leash with a tiny scrap of bright blue shag carpet on its end. She smiled. "Greetings, Cousin Horace. I think your Blat bat ears are pretty," she said. "It's nice to meet you."

Horace smiled back at her. "Uh, thanks," he said. "It's nice to meet you." He looked from her face to the patch of carpet on the floor. "Is that a pet shag rug?"

Aunt Myrtle smiled. "Cousin Crarpet gave it to Sugar. It's her first pet."

Sugar picked up the shag carpet and stroked it in her palm. The tiny strands of carpet waved at the Splattlys and Blattlys. "His name is Rugs," Sugar said.

Horace's mom rubbed her nose. "Achoo!" she sneezed. "Achoo!" Her eyes started tearing. "Oh, my! Achoo! Achoo!"

Nana Blattly wrinkled her nose. "Achoo! Achoo!"

Small red bumps appeared all over both ladies' faces.

Mrs. Splattly looked at the rug. "I-I'm sorry, Sugar, but can you please put your pet away? All Blattly women are allergic to hairy pets like that."

Aunt Myrtle wrinkled her brow. "This is my daughter's new pet, and she wants to show it to the family," she said.

Dr. Splattly stepped between Myrtle and Horace's mom. "I'm sure Sugar will keep Rugs away from the Blattly women. Right, Sugar?" he asked.

Sugar placed Rugs gently on the floor. "Uh-huh. I don't want anyone to feel bad," she said.

Horace stared at the shag rug pet. It looked just like the carpet covering the mall. Was Rugs growing? He'd have to keep a close eye on it all weekend long. "When is Cousin Crarpet getting here?" he asked. "I'd love to talk to him about these new pets."

Myrtle shook her head. "No, he can't come. He's too busy taking care of the Shag Shack," she said.

Just then Melody barged into the circle of family members. "Guess what?!" she announced. "The hotel forgot to give Horace his own room. He's going to have to share one with Sugar and me!"

A Room Without a View

Horace and Sugar looked out the room window. From the thirteenth floor, they could see boats sailing across Celernip Bay.

"Pretty great, huh?" Horace said.

"It's so pretty," Sugar said. She put Rugs on her shoulder.

Melody pushed her brother aside to stand beside her cousin. "Yes, Sugar, it is pretty. I totally agree," she said. "I like your new pet. Can I hold him?"

Sugar passed the shag rug to her cousin.

Melody took Rugs and petted the carpet. "Achoo! Achoo! Achoo!" she yelped, handing him back to Sugar. "I must be allergic like my mom." She looked at her hand. "Hey, the bottom of that thing is sticky." She sniffed it. "It's caramel."

Sugar nodded. "Uh-huh, that's what Cousin Crarpet said."

Horace brushed his hand across the top of Rugs. Strands of shag rug wrapped around his finger. "This thing is pretty strong," he said. He yanked hard, pulling his finger away.

"Achoo!" Melody sneezed. She walked to the bathroom and washed her hands. "Just keep him away from my side of the room, okay?"

Sugar set Rugs down on the windowsill. "I'll keep him over here," she said.

Horace turned and sat on the cot that the hotel staff had put in the room for him. The thin mattress felt as mushy and gross as cold oatmeal. Melody and Sugar went over and sat on their large bed. It looked as soft and comfy as a pile of whipped cream.

He eyed Rugs. The thing looked twice the size it had been when he'd first met Sugar in the hotel lobby. He picked up the phone and started to dial the number of Auggie and Xax Blootin. The Blootins were twins and Horace's best friends. The three boys were always investigating mysterious things that happened around Blootinville. They wrote all their mysteries in a notebook called *The Splattly and Blootin Big Book of Worldwide Conspiracies*.

While Horace dialed, Sugar opened her suitcase and took out a sketchpad. "Horace, is it all right if I draw some pictures of you with Rugs?"

Melody came out of the bathroom. "You want to draw pictures of *Horace*?" she asked. "Why him?"

"I think he has an interesting face," Sugar said.

Horace couldn't remember anyone ever wanting to draw him before. He hung up the phone, deciding to talk to the twins later. "Sure, that would be fun," he said. He reached into his suitcase and took out his new *Slimy Superhero* comic book. "I'll read this while you draw me."

Melody turned her head between her cousin and brother. "Sugar, what about me? You're supposed to play with *me*," she said. "Let's go ride the elevator and explore the hotel."

Sugar took out a box of colored pencils. "I'm going to draw Cousin Horace with Rugs," she said. "I can't leave my new pet alone, and since you're allergic, you can't be in the picture with Rugs."

Horace sat by the window and bit his lip to keep from laughing at his sister.

Melody folded her arms across her chest and marched to the door. "I thought we were going to be friends, Sugar, but I guess I was wrong." She stepped into the hall and slammed the door behind her.

Sugar looked at Horace, then made a few more lines on her paper. "I'm sorry your sister is allergic to Rugs, but why does she have to be so bossy and mean?" she asked.

Horace turned a page of his comic book.

"She just likes to be in charge all the time," he said. "But she really is very smart. She can invent really cool, scientific potions and stuff."

Sugar took out a black pencil and drew Horace's spiky hair. "Well, I prefer less bossy, quieter things," she said. "Like you and Rugs."

"Oh," Horace said. He had an itch on his knee but wasn't sure if he was allowed to move to scratch it or not. "Uh, is it okay if I—"

"Oh, my! Look!" Sugar said, pointing her pencil at the window. She laid her sketch pad down on the bed.

Horace moved his eyes to follow his cousin, being very careful not to turn his head or body. "Am I allowed to get up?" he asked.

Sugar laughed. "Of course," she said. She tapped her pencil on the glass. "The hotel has a big blue rug pet all over it."

Horace went to the window. Blue shag rug was quickly growing across the window, making the room as dark as if it were night.

"Isn't it cute?" Sugar asked. "I bet Cousin Crarpet sent it as a surprise for the family."

Horace switched on some lamps to brighten the room. "I think I'm going to try calling my friends again," he said. "Their dad's the mayor, so they get lots of information about stuff before even the newspaper does." Horace picked up the phone and dialed.

"Hello," Auggie answered on the phone in his room.

"Hello, hello," Xax answered on the phone in his room.

"Do you have to say 'hello' thirty-one times?" Auggie asked his brother.

"It's bad luck if I don't," Xax replied.

Horace sat up on the cot. "Listen, guys, it's me. I have something you need to help me investigate. There's this new blue shag rug pet and—"

"We have one," Auggie said.

"Your cousin Crarpet gave it to our dad," Xax said.

"Last night we put it in the basement, and

this morning, it was so big, the room was filled," Auggie said.

"Now we have it trapped down there, and we don't know what to do with it," Xax said.

"Do the police know anything?" Horace asked.

"Nope. No one does," Auggie said.

"Not even your cousin Crarpet," Xax said. "Our dad's really mad at him because the rug's invading the whole town."

Horace looked across the room at Rugs. "Okay, guys. Thanks for your help. If you get more info, call me at Hotel Stalagmite," he said.

"Will do," Auggie said. "See you."

"Bye, bye, bye, bye, bye, bye, bye, bye, bye, bye, bye, bye, bye, bye, bye, bye, bye, bye, bye, bye, bye, bye, bye, bye, bye, bye, bye, bye, bye, bye, bye, bye," Xax said.

Horace hung up the phone. Sugar had put Rugs on a leash and was dragging the carpet to the door.

"I'm going to go downstairs," Sugar told him.

"I think you better keep him in a suitcase so he doesn't get out of control," Horace told her.

"Nonsense," Sugar said. "He's very well behaved, and he'd be afraid in there." Before Horace could change his cousin's mind, Sugar had opened the door and left the room.

A REUNION DIVIDED

Over three hundred Splattlys and Blattlys sat at tables in the hotel's ballroom. The room's high ceiling was like the roof of a cave lit with stalactites. The floor was lit with lamps like stalagmites. Everyone ate dinner, laughed, and swapped stories. The parents talked about work and their homes. The kids talked about school, sports, and games they liked to play.

Horace sat at one of the kids' tables between Sugar and his great aunt's son's son's nephew.

Guy Blattly was seventeen and had long dirty hair and a pimple on his nose the size of a grape. He took a bite of his food, tossed his fork at his plate, and scrunched up his mouth. "This food stinks," he said.

Horace took a bite of his chicken. "I like it. The outside's sweet and tasty," he said. "What kind of stuff do you like? I like to investigate conspiracies. I think the shag rug pets are—"

Guy scrunched up his mouth. "Look, kid, I don't want to talk to you, so don't talk to me," he said.

Horace leaned away from Guy. He was even meaner than Melody when her lavender Lily Deaver emergency rope ladder had shrunk in the wash.

Melody smiled at Guy and leaned toward him. "My brother isn't very intelligent. He likes to do babyish things. I'm much more sophisticated than he is," she said.

Guy scrunched up his mouth. "Stop bothering me, *Smellody*," he said.

Melody dropped her smile and stared angrily at the teenager. "You're the rudest, most belligerent boy I've ever met," she said.

Sugar reached down to the floor to give Rugs a stroke. "Yes, that was terribly rude of you," she said to Guy.

"Oh, hush up, squirrel face," Guy said. He looked from Sugar to Melody and Horace. "Don't your moms hate each other because Aunt Myrtle liked her pet rabbit more than your mom?"

The cousins looked at one another. None of them knew what to say.

Guy grinned a large smile that made him look like a hungry wolf about to eat little children in the woods. He leaned over and picked Rugs off the floor. The pet was now the size of a doormat. Guy tossed him in the center of the table. "This is the dumbest pet ever," he said.

"Achoo!" Melody sneezed. "Achoo! Take that off the table now!"

Sugar tugged at the leash, but she couldn't get the rug to budge from the table. "He won't move. I think he likes it here," she said.

"Achoo!" Melody sneezed.

"Achoo!" Mrs. Splattly sneezed.

"Achoo!" Nana Blattly sneezed.

"Achoo! Achoo! Achoo!" Blattly women all around the room sneezed.

"What is making all the Blattly ladies sneeze?" someone asked.

Melody stood and waved a fork at Rugs. "Achoo! It's that awful pet rug that Cousin Crarpet Splattly made! All women who are Blattlys or part Blattly are allergic to pets!"

Mrs. Splattly stood. "Achoo! Well, then, we have to get rid of that pest!"

Sugar's lips trembled and her eyes filled with tears. "But I love my Rugs," she said.

"Achoo!" Nana Blattly sneezed.

Granny Splattly walked over to Sugar. "Rugs is my granddaughter's pet, and he stays!" she declared. "Crarpet Splattly made the rug pets, and we're proud of him!"

All the Splattlys cheered.

"It has to go!" Nana Blattly said. "Achoo!"

All the Blattlys cheered.

Aunt Myrtle shouted, "Blattly women are fakers! They sneeze and sniffle because they just don't like pets!"

Horace's mom shouted, "The Splattlys get pets just to make Blattly women sneeze! I bet Crarpet made the rug pets just to ruin this weekend for all the Blattlys!"

Splattlys and Blattlys stood at their tables yelling at one another. The adults pointed fingers and waved their hands in the air. The kids ran to their parents. Horace and Melody stood by Dr. and Mrs. Splattly's side. Sugar ran over and hid under her mom's skirt. Horace had never seen so many grown-ups so angry at one another.

Granny Splattly waved a stalk of celery in Nana Blattly's face. "Your family is a bunch of sniffling, nose-wiping babies!"

Nana Blattly waved a breadstick in Granny Splattly's face. "Your family likes making Blattly women sniffle and sneeze!"

The two women used their celery and bread-sticks like swords, leaning back and forth, poking each other in the nose.

"Achoo! Achoo! Achoo!" Sneezing was heard everywhere in the ballroom.

Blattly and Splattly men were pulling on Rugs like in a tug-of-war.

Horace, Melody, and Dr. and Mrs. Splattly stood by the wall. Horace wasn't sure whom to root for. His mother was a Blattly, and his dad was a Splattly. "Who do we want to win?" he asked.

"Who do we want to lose?" Melody asked.

Dr. and Mrs. Splattly looked down at their children. "We don't want anyone to win or lose," Dr. Splattly said.

"And no one's going to," Mrs. Splattly said. "I'm going to put a stop to this right now."

Crunch.

Nana Blattly batted her breadstick across Granny Splattly's nose. The breadstick broke in two, and Granny Splattly fell back against the table, sitting in a bowl of mashed celernips.

"I won!" Nana Blattly cheered.

The Blattly men wrapped Rugs up in a table-cloth and handed it to Sugar. "Keep him in here so he won't make the Blattly women sneeze," one of the Blattlys told her.

"I can't keep my pet in a tablecloth," Sugar said, crying.

"The reunion is over!" Granny Splattly yelled. "Everyone pack up and go home. The Splattly and Blattly families will never speak again!"

The Splattlys walked toward the east door of the ballroom to go back to their rooms and pack. The Blattlys walked toward the west door of the ballroom to go back to their rooms and pack.

The manager of the hotel ran onto the ball-room stage and picked up a microphone. "Everyone, stop!" he yelled. "Something terrible has happened!"

The Splattlys and Blattlys stopped.

"Is something wrong?" Horace asked, step-ping forward.

The manager nodded his head sadly. "I'm

orry to report that we're all trapped in the hotel. There's no getting out," he said.

"That's impossible!" Granny Splattly said. "There are lots of doors!"

"And lots of windows!" Nana Blattly said.

"Follow me," the manager said. He stepped off the stage and led everyone out of the room and into the hotel lobby. Blue shag carpeting blocked all the windows and doors on the outside of the hotel.

"Why is one of the pets covering the door?" Sugar asked.

Horace climbed up on the reception desk. "Listen up, everyone," he said. "Cousin Crarpet's pets are covering the town. I talked to the mayor's sons, and they told me their pet grew to fill the entire basement of Blootin Mansion."

Everyone gasped.

"Can't we just open the doors and windows and cut a hole?" Barney Blattly asked.

"If you open any doors and windows, it will grow in here and cover us," Horace explained.

All the Splattlys looked at Horace.

"How do we know you're telling the truth?" Myrtle asked. "You have Blattly blood in you just like your mother."

"My grandson is not a liar!" Nana Blattly said. "Cousin Crarpet made this awful pet, and now look what's happened!"

"Please, Mother, calm down," Mrs. Splattly told her mom, then she looked at the Splattly family. "If Horace said that's what's happening, then I'm sure it's true."

"But I love my Rugs," Sugar said.

Granny Splattly stomped her foot on the ground. "I don't care what's going on outside!" she yelled. "I'm not spending one more minute in this place with Blattlys!"

"Good riddance!" Nana Blattly yelled at her. "I hope the shag carpet swallows you up so I never have to see you again!"

Granny Splattly stuck out her tongue. "I hope the carpet covers the whole world so you sneeze forever!"

"Blattlys, let's get out of here!" Nana Blattly said.

"Don't do it!" Horace hollered.

No one listened. The Blattlys stormed toward the hotel entrance, but the second the automatic doors slid open, the Blattly women fell to the carpet sneezing and sneezing and sneezing. "Shut the doors!" Nana Blattly called, holding her nose.

Granny Splattly stepped over Nana Blattly. "If they won't leave, we will!" The Splattlys stepped to the hotel entrance, but the second the automatic doors slid open, the shag carpet creature grabbed at them. "Shut the doors!" Granny Splattly screamed.

The hotel doors slammed shut on the creature, saving the Splattlys. Little pieces of the rug lay on the floor, and hotel employees quickly swept them into garbage bags.

The Splattlys and Blattlys faced one another across the hotel lobby. They were trapped. Nana Blattly stared Granny Splattly in the eyes.

"Here's the plan: All Blattlys will stay on the top floors of the hotel, and all the Splattlys can stay in the rooms at the bottom," she said.

"Why do you get the top floors?" Granny Splattly said.

The hotel manager stepped between the two women. "How about all the Splattlys stay in rooms that end with the numbers one, three, five, seven, and nine, and all the Blattlys stay in rooms that end with the numbers two, four, six, and eight?"

"What about the rooms that end with zeroes?" Horace asked.

Mrs. Splattly put her hands on Horace's shoulders. "Since our family is a mix of Splattly and Blattly, we'll stay in two of those," she said.

Dr. Splattly put his hands on Melody's shoulders. "That's right. We refuse to be on either side. Horace and Melody will share one room that ends in a zero, and Mrs. Splattly and I will share another. The rest can be empty."

"Is that okay with everyone?" the hotel

manager asked Granny Splattly and Nana Blattly.

"That's fine with me," Nana Blattly said.

"That's fine with me, too," Granny Splattly said.

"What about Rugs?" Sugar asked.

Horace took the tablecloth holding Rugs from Sugar. "Just to be careful, the hotel manager can keep it in the big safe in the basement."

Sugar nodded. "Maybe just for the weekend," she said.

The hotel manager clapped his hands. "So do we agree on the plan?" he asked the two grandmothers.

The two old women stuck out their hands and shook. "Deal," they said. Then both women turned on their heels and headed up to their rooms.

No Way Out

Every floor of the hotel was divided in two by a thick line of red tape down the middle of each hallway. All the odd-number doors were on the right for the Splattlys, and all the even-number rooms were on the left for the Blattlys. The Blattlys walked down the right side of the hall calling the Splattlys "Evil rug-lovers." The Splattlys walked down the left side of the hall calling the Blattlys "Nasty sneezers."

Horace, Melody, and their parents straddled the line, putting one leg on one side and one leg on the other as Dr. and Mrs. Splattly walked

Horace and Melody to their kids' room at the far end of the hall on the twentieth floor.

"This is ridiculous," Mrs. Splattly said. "I wish we'd never had this reunion."

"This is awful," Melody said.

"I can't believe everyone's fighting about that stupid pet rug," Horace said.

Mrs. Splattly looked at Horace. "If Myrtle hadn't chosen Sniffles over me, there wouldn't be a problem," she said.

Dr. Splattly opened the room door. "I think

we've talked about this enough today," he said. The kids' parents walked out of the room, shutting the door behind them.

Horace sat on the end of his bed. The outside of the room's window was covered with blue shag carpet. "We have to come up with a plan to stop the carpet creature so we can all get out of here," he said.

"What can we do?" Melody asked. She switched on the TV. A news program showed pictures of the blue shag carpet covering Blootinville Elementary School, the *Blootinville Banner* skyscraper, and all of Society Hill where Auggie and Xax lived. The entire town looked like a big pile of blue shag carpet. A helicopter flew over the town, and a reporter leaned out the door with a microphone. "We're flying right over the Shag Shack," she said. "And this mound of carpet here is the maker of the rug pets, Mr. Crarpet Splattly." The reporter held the microphone in front of a pile of carpet that looked like a person.

"Are you okay in there?" the reporter asked.

The pile of carpet nodded and mumbled something.

The reporter held the microphone closer to the pile of carpet. "Can you speak up?" she asked. "We couldn't hear you." The rug grabbed the microphone from her hand, and the helicopter flew away.

Horace switched the TV off. "Do you think he's really okay in there?" he asked.

"I don't know," Melody said. "But what I do know is that we're trapped in here and there's nothing we can do."

Horace reached into his backpack and yanked out his Cupcaked Crusader costume. "Of course there's something we can do," he said. "You can make me a cupcake that will give me powers to destroy the shag carpet creature. Then all the Splattlys and Blattlys will be able to go home, and the town will be free again."

Melody flopped facedown on her bed. "Shrimp-o, I don't have any ingredients to make cupcakes."

Horace pointed to the window. "But we have to do something," he said. "If we don't, we may be trapped in here forever."

Melody sat up on the bed. "Okay. Well, I'd need a sample to test, and Rugs is locked in the safe."

Horace took two strands of bright blue shag rug out of his pocket. "Will this do?" he asked. "I got it off the lobby floor when the sliding doors closed." He unzipped his suitcase, dumped his clothes out, then tossed in the pieces. The small strands of carpet wriggled around inside and immediately began growing.

Horace slapped his suitcase shut and opened the room door. "Now let's get to work," he said.

• • •

Late that night, two Splattly children were hard at work in the hotel's giant kitchen. Everyone else in the hotel had gone to sleep hours before. The kitchen had five huge ovens, four mixing bowls that were even taller than Horace, and had enough counter space to cover the Splattly's front and back yards. Plus it had a dishwasher that was big enough to hold a car! All Horace had to do was slide dishes in the door on one side and a couple seconds later they came out a door on the other side completely clean.

Slam! Whoosh! Slam! Whoosh! "Look how good it cleans," Horace said. "Wouldn't it be great to take baths in one of these?" He held his suitcase in one hand and pushed the dishwasher's buttons with the other.

Melody held a jar of mushrooms up to the light. "You could help me look for ingredients," she said.

Horace tossed the suitcase down by the dishwasher and walked across the room. "What should I look for?" he asked.

Melody pointed at the flour, sugar, and eggs in a small mixing bowl. "I have the stuff to make regular cupcakes, but I need my special ingredients." She went over to the suitcase. "Hmmmm . . . But I do have one idea." Melody flipped the suitcase open. The shag carpet had grown to cover the entire inside. A big piece reached out to grab her.

Horace ran over. "Hey! Watch what you're doing!"

Melody slid the suitcase into the dishwasher and slammed the door shut. She pressed the *ON* button, and the machine *whooshed* with crashing waves of water. Then she pushed the *OFF* button, opened the dishwasher, and slid out the suitcase.

The shag carpet was flat, soggy, and soapy. The rug tried to wriggle, but it was too heavy and full of water. Melody slammed the suitcase shut and reached under the large kitchen's sink. "Now I know *exactly* the kind of cupcakes to make," she said.

● ● ●

"Are you sure this will work?" Horace asked. He stood in the hotel lobby wearing his Cupcaked Crusader outfit. He looked at the door, which was completely covered by the shag carpet creature.

"Of course it will work," Melody said. She handed her brother two identical cupcakes. "I found enough stuff in the kitchen to make two superpowered cupcakes. Eat one now so you can get home and get my special ingredients, then eat the second cupcake so you can come back here."

Horace stuck one cupcake in the pocket in the wing of his outfit. He looked at the other cupcake he held in his hand. It was big, white, and glittered like snow on a sunny day. He sniffed it. It didn't smell. Not sweet, not sour, not anything.

"Just eat it," Melody said.

Horace turned to his sister. "What will you tell Mom and Dad if I'm not back before it's morning?"

Melody shrugged. "I'll say you're playing in another part of the hotel with Sugar," she said.

Horace nodded. "Sounds good," he answered. He opened his mouth, stuck in the cupcake, and chewed.

The cupcake didn't taste good. But it didn't

taste bad either. It tasted light, fluffy, and dry, like he was eating Styrofoam. Horace swallowed the cupcake. His stomach got warm and sloshy like the inside of a washing machine. The sloshing reached up from his stomach into the back of his throat.

Horace felt as if he was going to be sick. He put his hand over his mouth and turned to run for the bathroom.

Melody grabbed him and pushed him toward the hotel's entrance. The automatic doors slid open, and the shag carpet creature reached in to grab the Cupcaked Crusader.

"Now!" Melody yelled.

Horace opened his mouth, and a gigantic wave of soapy, bubbly water crashed out and slammed into the shag carpet. The shag rug fell to the ground, lying there like a giant, wet towel.

Horace looked at his sister. "Did I kill the rug that was on the door?" he asked.

Melody stepped forward. "No, it's only too soggy to get us. On your way home, soap and

soak the carpet so you can walk over it. Get my ingredients, eat the second soapy cupcake, and hurry back here. Make sure you're back in the hotel before the sun comes up. Once the shag carpet dries and your powers run out, the carpet will be able to get you."

Horace felt his stomach bubbling and frothing with soapy, warm water. He stepped out of the hotel and onto the rug he'd already soaked. Bright blue shag carpet was everywhere. It glowed and wriggled in the moonlight, covering the cars in the parking lot, the streetlights on the roads, and every building, tree, and boat in sight. The Cupcaked Crusader walked across the soggy carpet until he got to a spot where the carpet was dry. The shag grabbed for Horace's legs.

Brawp.

The Cupcaked Crusader spewed hot, soapy water from his mouth, flattening the evil carpet to mush.

SHRINK CITY

Horace soaked the shag carpet, stepped over it, and got closer and closer to home. Along the way, he saw a familiar-shaped pile of shag carpet, soaked it, and found a bicycle underneath. He climbed on it and pedaled through Blootinville, splattering soapy water out of his mouth and clearing a path to the Splattly home.

The town was so quiet that it felt as if Blootinville were a ghost town.

But Horace knew that wasn't true. He knew

that inside all these homes and stores, people were trapped and couldn't get out because of the shag carpet.

The other thing Horace noticed was that everything looked as if it were just a little bit shorter than it used to be.

The flagpole in front of Blootinville Elementary was covered with shag carpet and looked about a foot shorter than it had the day before.

Blootinville Mall should have been about fifteen feet high. Tonight it looked only ten feet tall.

The street sign for Hill Hop Toad was closer to the ground, and the fountain outside Penny Honey's home had shrunk, too. Usually it had a big gold mermaid holding a big golden fish. Now it was covered with carpet, and it looked like a baby holding a guppy.

The shag carpet was squeezing everything and making it smaller!

If Horace didn't stop it, would the shag carpet squeeze all the homes and buildings until they were as small as dollhouses? What would happen to the people inside?

Horace looked at the Splattly home. Every window and door was covered, just like all the other homes in town. He spewed a wave of water across the lawn of his home and walked up to the front door. The doorknob used to be at the same height as his chest. Now it was only as high as his waist.

Horace spat on the door, got the shag carpet to lie on the ground, and opened the door. He stepped inside the dark house and shut the door behind him. He could feel the soapy sick feeling in his stomach go away. He'd made it home just as his powers had run out.

He switched on a lamp in the hallway and looked at the clock in the hallway. The time was four twenty-nine in the morning. He had to work fast. Horace went into the living room, picked up the cordless phone, lay back on the couch, and dialed. He knew it was late, but there were two people he had to talk to.

"Uh, who is this?" a sleepy Xax answered.

"Wha—Hello?" a sleepy Auggie answered.

Horace could see the ceiling very slowly growing closer to the ground. When he looked at the walls, he could see them slowly growing closer together.

"Hey," he told his friends. "Have you found out anything about the shag carpet that could help me get rid of it?" he asked.

"Is it thirty-one o'clock?" Xax asked.

"Is this a wrong number?" Auggie asked.

"Why isn't there ever a thirty-one o'clock?" Xax asked.

"WAKE UP!" Horace shouted. "I need your help, or the town will be completely destroyed!"

Auggie yawned into the phone. "Horace, if my dad knew how to make it go away, don't you think he would?" he asked.

"Yeah," Xax said. "All he told us was that the police used special listening stuff and heard the carpet whispering that it was very, very hungry and always wanted to eat."

"And that they think its weakness may be the caramel padding on the bottom. It's—"

The phone went dead. Horace clicked redial. Nothing happened. There wasn't even a dial tone. The rug must have cut the phone lines.

He climbed upstairs, turning on lights as he went. He sat at Melody's lavender Lily Deaver desk and stuck the forefinger of his right hand in his ear and the forefinger of his left hand on his chin, getting into his thinking pose. He tried to remember all the things he'd learned about the shag carpet.

1. The shag carpet's caramel padding may be its weakness.
2. The shag carpet was hungry and making all the buildings get smaller.
3. The shag carpet could whisper.
4. The phone didn't work anymore.

The lights in the house suddenly went dark. Horace switched Melody's desk lamp off and on. Nothing happened. He picked Melody's radio off her desk. It wouldn't go on either. The shag rug had cut off the electricity.

Horace sat in the dark and finished making his list.

5. The electricity didn't work anymore.
6. The only person left who could save Blootinville was the Cupcaked Crusader!

Horace stumbled across the dark room, walked into a shelf, and felt his way around the walls of the room until he bumped into his sister's Lily Deaver coatrack. He took her Lily Deaver tote bag off a hook, then got down on his hands and knees and crawled across the floor, feeling his way to Melody's Lily Deaver Spill & Brew Science Laboratory. His sister made all her own ingredients for the cupcakes and kept them in small jars under the lab. She had over two hundred small jars on four long shelves. Horace had seen them before and knew the jars had all sorts of weird stuff in them. One jar had fly wings, one was filled with toenail clippings, one was packed with dust, and another was filled with a mixture of eyelashes, banana peels, and cod liver oil. Other jars had stuff that Horace couldn't even identify.

But that didn't matter. Horace just reached out to the shelves and stuffed as many of the jars as he could fit into Melody's tote bag. He zipped it closed, slung the bag over his shoulder, and stood up. He took the other cupcake out and quickly ate it.

Now all he had to do was get back to Hotel Stalagmite before the sun came up and dried the shag carpet.

Chapter 9

SPEAKING SHAG

Horace climbed on the bicycle and burped up waves of soapy water as he pedaled across town. The ride back to the hotel went slower than Horace's ride home. He was feeling more tired, not to mention he was also carrying the heavy tote bag full of Melody's ingredients.

Horace's tongue hung from his mouth, and his eyelids dropped. Soapy water kept splashing up into his nose, making it hard to breathe. He poked his eyes with his fingers and looked at all the houses and apartment buildings along the streets. He had to stay awake! People were inside those houses and buildings and needed his help!

A sliver of orange sun appeared on the horizon. In a few minutes, it would sit high in the sky and the carpet would start drying. Then the rug would be able to grab him.

Horace pedaled faster, spitting soapy water as hard as he could. The sun rose, changing from a dull orange to a bright yellow. Horace turned his head and saw that the patch of shag rug he'd just spit on was already drying. The shag wiggled to grab the bicycle.

The hotel was only one hundred more yards. Once inside, he'd be safe and Melody would have her ingredients to make cupcakes so Horace could defeat the shag carpet for good.

Horace leaned over the handlebars and opened his mouth to let out one last wave of soapy water.

Nothing fell out but his tongue.

Horace shut his mouth then opened it again. Still nothing.

His powers were gone.

The shag rug creature grabbed the bike tires, stopping Horace from pedaling. The carpet began creeping up toward Horace's feet.

The Cupcaked Crusader may not have had his powers, but he still had his brains! Horace climbed up and stood on the bicycle, balancing one foot on the handlebars and the other on the seat.

The shag reached higher, tickling the bottoms of Horace's feet.

Horace remembered what Auggie and Xax had told him. They said that the police had heard the shag carpet whispering. This meant that if the shag carpet could talk, then maybe it could listen, too!

Horace had his answer. He would talk to the carpet so it would let him get back inside the hotel.

The shag carpet wrapped around Horace's

ankles and tried to pull him off the bike. Horace looked down at the rug and spoke. "Hey!" he yelled. "Stop that or I won't give you anything to eat!"

He watched the carpet. It let go of his ankles. Horace kept talking. "If you stop grabbing me and let me ride my bike into the hotel, then I'll let you inside and my sister can make you lots of food. She's a very good cook. If you want, you can eat her, but I don't think she'd taste very good," he joked.

The carpet slid down and let go of the bicycle wheels.

Horace sat on the bicycle seat. "Great! We have a deal," he said.

The carpet waved to Horace and folded back like two giant waves, revealing solid ground. Horace pedaled along the path between the two walls of carpet. When he reached the hotel doors, he leapt off the bike and stepped inside the hotel. Because the electricity had gone out, he had to push the automatic doors shut behind him before the rug could get in.

"Ha!" he laughed, grinning at the shag rug. "Loser!"

The carpet rose high in the air and crashed against the doors. The hotel shook, but the doors held.

"*Yes!*" Horace said, pumping his fists in the air. "The Cupcaked Crusade always wins!"

Chapter 10

303 CUPCAKES

"You stay on your side!"

"You stay on yours!"

"Sneezer snotters!"

"Evil rug lovers!"

Horace woke to the sound of shouting from the hall. He sat up in bed, grabbed a flashlight off his night table, and shined it at his watch. It was nine-thirty in the morning. He'd gotten back to the hotel at six-thirty and had had only three hours of sleep. He stretched his arms, looking around the room.

Melody was nowhere to be seen. Nor was her Lilly Deaver lavender tote bag with the ingredients Horace had brought from home.

Horace stood. The walls of the room crept in at him a tiny bit. The ceiling crept lower. It was probably almost two feet shorter than it was yesterday when the reunion had begun. He brushed his teeth, dressed, and headed into the hallway with his flashlight, making sure he kept one leg on either side of the red tape that ran down the middle of the hall so no one would think he liked the Splattlys or Blattlys better.

Downstairs, another line of red tape divided the dining room. The Splattly family sat on one side, the Blattly family on the other. The room was lit with candles. One table sat directly on top of the line. That was Horace's family's table. Horace took a seat. His dad's hair drooped over his face, and he had stubble on his cheeks. A crust of toast hung over his lip. His mom's hair curled over her eyes. She stared at a hard-boiled egg rolling across her plate.

"Uh, what's the matter?" he asked.

"We didn't sleep well," Dr. Splattly said. "Nana Blattly and Granny Splattly said we have to choose which side we're on."

"This is awful," Mrs. Splattly said.

"I wish Cousin Crarpet had never made those pet rugs," Dr. Splattly said, patting his wife's hand.

Horace looked around the room. "Where's Melody?" he asked.

"In the kitchen," Dr. Splattly said. "She's baking special breakfast treats for everyone."

Horace stood. What was his sister up to? "I'll go see if she needs my help," he said. Just as he was walking into the kitchen, a line of ten waiters marched into the dining room. Each held a large tray of cupcakes. All the cupcakes were striped purple and green, and in the center of each was a sparkly sugar jewel.

Horace entered the kitchen to find Melody facing a tall, thin man wearing a chef's hat. She waved a finger in his face. "I told you the cup-

cakes weren't ready yet. I made a mistake and need them back!" she yelled.

The chef waved a hand in Melody's face. "The cupcakes are splendid! Leave me alone!" He walked off to another part of the kitchen.

Melody stood holding a plate of three cupcakes. One cupcake was dark green and looked like moldy cheese. Another was so clear it looked like it was made out of glass. The third looked exactly like the ones that were on the trays the waiters had carried into the dining room.

"What's going on?" he asked. "Why'd you make so many cupcakes?"

Melody took a deep breath. "The chef wouldn't let me use the kitchen just to make three cupcakes for you. He said I had to make cupcakes for everyone."

Horace picked up the plate with the three cupcakes. "So? You made three for my superpowers. We're all set. What's the problem?" he asked.

Melody shook her head. She pointed a finger at the small moldy cupcake and the glass cupcake. "See these? These cupcakes are for you," she said. She picked up the striped cupcake. "But I also made you one superpower cupcake that looks exactly like all the ones the waiters are serving."

"What's wrong with that?" Horace asked.

Melody bit into the striped cupcake, chewed, and swallowed. "This *isn't* the superpower cupcake. One of the waiters took your cupcake and got it mixed up with all the other ones. Now someone out there is about to eat it, and I don't know who."

Horace ran to the kitchen door. "Then why are we standing here? We have to stop everyone," he said.

Melody placed her hands on her hips. "How are we supposed to stop three hundred people from eating three hundred cupcakes and find out which one has the superpowers?" she asked. She tore a piece of foil off the roll, wrapped the two superpower cupcakes up, and tucked them in her tote bag.

Horace took her arm. "Maybe it's not too late," he said. "We can't let someone eat it." He dashed into the dining room and saw three hundred people licking the last bits of purple frosting and green frosting from their fingertips. There wasn't one cupcake anywhere to be seen.

Melody stood beside Horace and shrugged. "I can't help it if I'm such a great baker that everyone eats my cupcakes so fast."

Horace looked at his sister. "I can't believe you let this happen," he said. "It's going to take a lot of powers to defeat this shag carpet creature. It covers the whole town."

Melody leaned over her brother. "Listen up, shortcake. We're lucky enough the ovens run on gas, not electricity. And, it's not my fault you took so long getting back here from home. If you'd come sooner, I could have baked your cupcakes before the chef had woken up."

Horace held his tongue. There was no point

in arguing with his sister. It would only make her madder. "Uh, do you have a plan for what happens when someone starts getting the super-powers?" he asked.

Melody tossed her hair back. "Maybe no one will get superpowers," she answered. "I only make the cupcakes to work for you, so it may not work on anyone else."

"But how do you know for sure?" Horace asked.

Melody folded her arms across her chest and looked at the room full of Splattlys and Blattlys. "I'll worry about that if and when it happens," she said.

Across the room, Sugar all of a sudden shut her eyes and snapped her fingers. Her face instantly turned green. Sugar snapped her fingers again. Her face instantly turned purple.

"Time to start worrying," Horace told his sister.

Chapter 11

HIDING THE EGGPLANT

Sugar snapped her fingers again, and her face turned green. She snapped again, and her face turned purple.

Melody nodded. "Hmmmm . . . That's exactly what I thought it would do to you," she said. "I guess my cupcakes do work on other people." She reached into her tote bag, pulled out her notebook, and wrote down some numbers.

"Can't you do that later?" Horace asked. "We have to get her out of here." He yanked a tablecloth off an empty table, sending plates, glasses, and silverware crashing to the floor.

"Horace, what are you doing?!" Mrs. Splattly asked.

"Sugar, what's wrong?" Aunt Myrtle asked. "Why are you changing colors?"

Sugar kept snapping, changing her face over and over and over.

Horace tossed the tablecloth over her head. "Oh, uh, this is all just part of a game we're playing," he said. He took Sugar's hand and began walking her to the elevators.

Aunt Myrtle stepped in front of him. "What kind of game?"

Horace laughed. "Sugar's pretending to be an—uh—eggplant! They're purple, aren't they?"

"Then why is she also turning green?" Aunt Myrtle asked.

Melody took Sugar's other hand. "That's because she's also pretending to be broccoli. Horace and I are going to deliver her to the vegetable market!"

Sugar stood under the tablecloth, snapping her fingers. Horace and Melody led her toward the stairway. "What a good eggplant," Horace said.

"What a good broccoli," Melody said.

Aunt Myrtle watched them leave. "I've never heard of a game like that before," she said.

• • •

A few minutes later, Horace and Melody stood in their room watching Sugar snap her fingers and change her face from purple to green over and over and over.

Melody placed her tote bag on the bed and took out her notebook. "Very interesting. I didn't think the snapping would last so long," she said.

"Do you think Sugar knows what's going on?" Horace asked.

"I don't think so," Melody answered.

Horace circled his color-changing cousin. "Will she get powers like I do?"

Melody wrote some math equations on a piece of paper. "We'll have to see, won't we?"

Horace leaned into Sugar's face. "Aren't you worried about what will happen if she gets powers?"

Melody pushed Horace aside. "Don't worry yourself. I'll take care of that."

"You better," Horace said. He gazed at the window covered with shag carpet. "We have to stop this." He reached into the tote bag and took out the two cupcakes his sister had made. "Which one do I eat first?" He went over to his backpack and took out his Cupcaked Crusader costume.

Melody kept her eyes on Sugar. "Eat the big cupcake first. That will start you off. Then keep the other one in your pocket to eat one hour later. That will be the perfect time for you to defeat the shag carpet. And make sure you eat it with a glass of Blootinberry juice."

Horace slapped his head. "I have to eat the cupcake with *Blootinberry juice*? How am I supposed to get Blootinberry juice while I'm fighting an evil carpet? I can't just tell the rug to wait for me to come back while I run to the store."

Melody put her hands on Sugar's shoulders and sat her on the bed. "I did the best I could with the ingredients you brought me," she told her brother. "And one more thing—it has to be *fresh-squeezed* Blootinberry juice."

"Fresh-squeezed! Can't I just get some from a carton?" Horace asked.

His sister rolled her eyes. "No! Just get some Blootinberries and squeeze out the juice. Don't be so lazy."

Horace frowned. "I'll go change into my superhero costume and eat the first cupcake," he said. He picked up the cupcakes and walked into the bathroom, shutting the door behind him.

A superhero had to make fresh-squeezed Blootinberry juice to get powers?! *Ridiculous!*

Horace stepped into his Cupcaked Crusader costume, tucked the small cupcake in the pocket of his wing, then unwrapped the larger

cupcake. It looked and felt just like glass. How would he ever be able to bite into it? Would it splinter and cut him?

"Are you sure this is okay to eat?" he called through the door.

"Of course!" Melody yelled.

Horace put the cupcake to his mouth and sunk his teeth into it—*crrrrackkkk*—Horace's teeth broke through the hard shell of the cupcake then—*ploof*—the cake exploded in his mouth into a puff of sweet, cool air. The strong breeze blew through his mouth, and it spread through his body. From the tips of his fingers to the soles of his feet, through every hair on his head, it was as if a windy day were whipping through him. The wind blasted through his arms and legs, exploded in his lungs, and swirled through his brain, getting louder and louder until two clouds burst from his ears.

Horace took a deep breath, feeling better now that the wind had stopped. He took a look in the bathroom mirror.

Horace squinted and leaned in, examining his appearance. Something was wrong. He didn't look at all like he usually did when he was the Cupcaked Crusader.

No, this time, he was barely there at all.

Almost a Ghost

Horace looked at himself in the mirror. Instead of seeing the Cupcaked Crusader looking back at him, he saw what looked like *a ghost* of the Cupcaked Crusader. He could see right through himself to the bathtub behind him! And he wasn't standing on the floor, but was floating one inch above it.

He held a hand to his eyes and wiggled his fingers. He could move them, but he could also see through them. He poked himself in the stomach, and his hand reached through himself and out his back.

Horace nudged the bathroom door with a toe. Could he walk through it? At first, it felt as if he couldn't, but when he pushed a bit harder, his whole body slid through the door. For a second, everything went black, then he came out on the other side and was floating in the hotel room.

"Whoa! Look at me!" he shouted with a laugh.

"Whoa! Look at me!" Sugar Splattly answered.

Horace floated in midair and stared at his cousin. Sugar's face had returned to normal, and she was bouncing up and down on the bed. But that wasn't the weird part. What was weird was that she was dressed in a bright yellow superhero outfit just like his!

"Do you like it?" Sugar asked. "Melody made it for me out of one of the bedspreads. She sews really fast. Take a look at the name she gave me!" She spun in a circle. Across the back of the costume were large orange letters spelling out Sugar's new superhero name: THE ANNIHILATOR.

Melody faced the window. The shag carpet creature pressed against it.

Horace called to his sister, pointing to his body. "Was this supposed to happen?"

Melody turned to look at her brother. "That's exactly as I'd planned. I've changed your body chemistry so you're lighter than air. You'll be able to interact with the shag carpet creature, but the shag carpet creature won't be able to grab you."

Horace smiled. "So can I just float out of here and start rolling up the rug?" he asked.

"Hardly," Melody answered. "The caramel padding on the bottom makes it nearly impossible to pull up."

"Will I be able to help?" Sugar asked. "I don't feel like I have powers."

Horace floated over to his sister. "Maybe I should head out on my own," he said.

"Just watch this," Melody said. She lifted the window an inch.

"Don't!" Horace yelled.

Melody flung the window as wide as she could and stepped aside. The shag carpet reached inside, clinging to Sugar with hundreds of its shaggy strands.

"Fight it off, Annihilator," Melody told her. "I know you can."

"I'm too weak and little," Sugar said.

"Do it!" Melody ordered.

Sugar reached up and grabbed the carpet in her hands, tearing it off her body. She yanked the blue shag from the caramel padding and tossed the padding out the window. Then she tied the shag strands into a long braid. When another piece of carpet tried to get in, she twisted that into rope and knotted it to the end of the first piece.

"Amazing!" Horace said.

"She has super strength," Melody explained.

"And I'm a naturally gifted ponytail braider," Sugar said. She tore more and more strands of carpet off the caramel bottom and knotted them together into one long rope. When no more carpet tried to get into the room, she tied one end of the carpet to the bed and tossed the rope out the window. She smiled. "Being a superhero is even more fun than playing with dolls!" she said.

Horace looked out the window. The long rope of rug carpet hung down to the ground. Now that the window was clear, he could see all of Blootinville covered with shag carpet. Everything had grown just a little bit smaller. "Since Sugar has powers to destroy the carpet, why can't she just tear it all up?" he asked.

Melody picked up a small patch of caramel padding that Sugar hadn't tossed out the window. "Sugar can tear the shag off the back of the rug, but take a look at this," she said.

Horace and Sugar leaned over Melody's hand. New, baby strands of shag rug were sprouting.

"It grows back," Sugar said. "How cute and evil."

"That's why you have the second cupcake,"

Melody said. "Use the powers you have now to get to the center of town for Blootinberry juice. Then eat the second cupcake to defeat the rug before it shrinks the buildings so small we'll be crawling around on our hands and knees."

Horace threw one leg over the windowsill and climbed out, grabbing hold of the shag rug rope.

Melody put her hand on his hand. "And don't waste your time saving Sara Willow," she instructed.

Horace scowled. "*I'm* the Cupcaked Crusader. I'll save *who* I want *when* I want," he said, shimmying down the rope.

Sugar followed after Horace. "Don't worry," she whispered to Melody. "I'll keep him in line."

"I'm counting on it," Melody said, shutting the window.

Horace slid lower and lower, bouncing his feet off the side of the hotel like he'd seen climbers do down the sides of mountains. The carpet on the hotel kept grabbing at him. It tickled his body, but it flicked right through, unable to catch him. Whenever the shag tried to grab Sugar, she kicked it with a foot, sending the shag flying into the air.

Horace dropped to the ground and floated above the shag carpet. Sugar landed beside her cousin, bent over, and tore up a long strip of carpet, clearing a path to walk along. "Now what do we do?" she asked.

Horace got down on his hands and knees and reached deep inside the carpet to the bottom. He felt the soft caramel pad that all the little pieces of shag rug were attached to. He pushed harder and harder until his body slid into the rug. Everything got dark. The rug tickled him inside and outside his body. When the tickling stopped, he found himself under the rug with the pad on top of him. It felt sticky, and he had to keep crawling under it so it wouldn't stick to him.

"Hey! What are you doing?" Sugar asked.

Horace poked his head back through the rug.

"Hold on a second; I want to try something," he told her. Horace ducked his head back under, opened his mouth, and took a bite of the rug pad. It was caramel! Sweet, chewy caramel! It tasted so good that Horace took two more bites.

Holes appeared where he had taken his bites, and the sun shone down on his face. The shag rug pieces that had been attached to the caramel fell across his cheek. Horace brushed them away.

"You stopped it," Sugar said. "It's not moving or growing anymore."

Horace floated above the carpet. "Auggie and Xax said that caramel padding is the rug's weakness," he said. "Let's head into town, make some fresh Blootinberry juice, eat the cupcake, and see what happens."

He raised a fist to his cousin. "The Cupcaked Crusader and the Annihilator unite to destroy the shag carpet creature!" he cheered.

Sugar wrinkled her nose. "But not Rugs," she said.

Horace looked at his cousin. She may be the strongest little girl in the world, but that didn't mean she still wasn't his sweet, young cousin. "We'll try and figure out a way to keep Rugs," he told her. "How does that sound?"

Sugar smiled, raised her fist, and knocked it against Horace's fist. "To the defeat of the shag rug creature but not Rugs!" she said.

Chapter 13

WHICH WHAT IS WHERE?

The Cupcaked Crusader and the Annihilator walked up and down every street. Where were they going to find fresh Blootinberries so they could make juice?

"I don't see any supermarkets," Sugar said. She tore up another strip of carpet so she could walk across the ground.

Horace floated around her. "Everything looks the same because it's covered with shag rug," he said.

"Wait!" Sugar exclaimed, stopping in her tracks. She pointed to a pile of rug. "I think this lump is the same shape as Mrs. Pyrzk's Fresh Fruit and Shoelace Depot. I come here all the time when I want orange rubber shoelaces for my waterproof hiking slippers. Step through the wall and get the juice."

Horace looked at the lump of carpet. It looked exactly the same as all the other piles of carpet on the street. "Are you sure?" he asked.

Sugar pouted. "Just because I'm in second grade and you're in fourth grade doesn't mean I can't be a smart superhero," she said.

"You're right," Horace said. "Hold on. I'll be right back." He stepped through the shag carpet and into the shop.

But he didn't find fresh fruit and shoelaces.

What he saw was Chef Quaquaqua taking a spaghetti-and-meatball bath by candlelight.

The school cafeteria chef's eyes went wide, and he let out a scream. "It's the ghost of the Cupcaked Crusader! The shag rug creature

caught him!" he shrieked. "We're doomed! We're all doomed!" He jumped out of the bathtub, splattering spaghetti sauce everywhere. He grabbed a towel, wrapping it around his waist.

"I'm not a ghost!" Horace told the chef in his Cupcaked Crusader voice. "I'm using superpowers so the shag carpet creature can't get me."

The chef smiled. "Are you here to save me?" he asked. "I've been stuck in my home for a whole day."

"I'm going to save the whole town," Horace answered.

Chef Quaquaqua stuck out his hand. It was covered with sauce, and meatballs were stuck on the tips of his fingernails. "It's a pleasure to meet you," he said. "Good luck defeating the shag carpet."

Horace stared at the chef's fingers and folded his hands behind his back. "Uh, I have to go right now. Sorry, I don't have time to shake your hand." He stepped through the wall to the outdoors.

"We have to be more careful which buildings I step into," he told Sugar.

"That wasn't the shoelace market?" she asked. "Whoopsa-daisy! Sorry about that."

Horace laughed. "No problem," he said. He didn't tell his cousin what he'd seen in there. She was too young to hear stories about Chef Quaquaqua taking a bath in spaghetti and meatballs.

"Where should we go next? You choose this time," Sugar said.

Horace looked to his left and right. "Do you think Mrs. Pyrzk's store is farther down the street," he asked.

She licked the back of a piece of rug, tasting the caramel. "I'm not sure I remember which building it is," she said.

"We'll just have to take our chances," Horace said. The duo strolled down the street. Horace stopped in front of a pile of carpet in the shape of a building. "Should I try this one?" he asked.

Sugar grabbed the rug and tore a piece off the building. The paint underneath the rug was bright pink. "This could be it," she said.

Horace nodded. "Okay, here goes," he said. He stepped through the wall and into the building.

What he saw was a woman in a smock, a pig in a sparkly gold wig, and people sitting in barbershop chairs. The room was lit with candles.

Everyone shrieked, "The shag carpet creature turned the Cupcaked Crusader into a little ghost!"

The pig snorted and hid behind a curtain.

Horace had entered Madame Chantilly

Bellray's House of Beauty. "I'm not a ghost," he said in his low Cupcaked Crusader voice. "I'm still a superhero."

Madame Chantilly Bellray clapped her hands. "The Cupcaked Crusader is here to save us," she said.

A man in a chair sat up. He looked exactly like a walrus. Horace recognized him as Mr. Howlly, the doughnut maker. "Thank goodness," Mr. Howlly said. "I came in to get my hairdo like a powdered sugar doughnut and have been trapped all night."

Tammy Biddy and Cleo Bumratt sat in two chairs. Their hair was wrapped in piles of curlers. They were third graders from Blootinville Elementary.

"I have to go home and get ready for my birthday party," Tammy said.

Cleo leaned over to the superhero and whispered, "I have to get home and wrap my gift for Tammy. I got her a combination Lily Deaver trash can and ballroom gown."

Madame Chantilly Bellray took the Cupcaked

Crusader's hands. "Please, help us get out. The shop keeps getting smaller, and all we've had to eat since yesterday are a box of crackers and some of Wiggles's pig chow."

Wiggles stuck his head out from behind the curtain and snorted. Obviously he didn't like having to share his meals.

Horace floated on top of the counter. "Okay, everyone, I promise to save you very shortly."

Tammy looked at her Lilly Deaver combination wristwatch and freckle stretcher. "Will I get to have my birthday party?" she asked. "It's at three o'clock. If you save us in time, I'll invite you," she said. "We're going to have mashed celernip cake with radish icing."

Horace backed toward the wall. "Uh, I'll see what I can do," he said. He stepped through the wall and back into the sunlight.

He couldn't waste any more time talking to people in the wrong homes or buildings. The shag carpet creature was making everything smaller, and soon no one would be able to stand up inside anymore. Thinkthinkthink, Horace thought. Where was Mrs. Pyrzk's Fresh Fruit and Shoelace Depot?

Then suddenly he realized someone was missing.

Sugar! The Annihilator!

She was nowhere to be seen! Horace looked behind him. "Sugar! Where are you?! Sugar!" he screamed.

He spun around in every direction. Where had she gone? Was she playing hide-and-seek? "Sugar, quit fooling around. Where are you?"

"Mmmm-hrrrrr . . . hlllp. . . ," a small pile of rug said. A second later, some of the shag fell to the ground and a mouth appeared.

Horace looked at the mouth. "Sugar?" he asked.

"Yes, it's me," she answered. Her mouth chewed off more of the caramel padding. Shag fell to the ground, and more of her face appeared. "My powers ran out and the carpet covered me," she said.

"Are you okay?" Horace asked.

"Yes, but the rug keeps growing back, and my stomach's almost full," she said. "Did you find Blootinberry juice?"

Horace shook his head. "Not yet, but I will right now." He started to float down the street.

"Wait!" Sugar called. "I remember which building it is." She stuck out her tongue and pointed two buildings down from the beauty salon. "That's the place. I'm positive."

Horace wasn't sure if she really was right or not, but he figured he should give it a try. "Great!" he said, trying to sound as if he believed her. "I'll be back as fast as I can!"

Horace floated forward, counted down two buildings, and stepped into the small mound of shag.

Candles lit the room in a soft orange glow. Behind a counter sat a fat woman. She was sleeping with her head resting on an old-fashioned cash register. While she slept, she tied shoelaces with one hand and peeled apples with the other.

Sugar was right! He'd found Mrs. Pyrzk's Fresh Fruit and Shoelace Depot!

A small bell on the counter had a sign in front of it that read, PLEASE, RING FOR SERVICE.

Horace gave the bell a shake.

Ding-a-ling-a-ling.

The woman woke, slamming back in her chair with her eyes wide. Shoelaces flew out of one hand and soared straight through Horace's forehead. "Ouch!" he cried. Apple peels sailed out of her other hand and flew through Horace's cheek. "Eeee-yuck!" he cried. Even though he was almost invisible, he could still feel the stuff go through him.

The woman leaned over the counter. "Welcome," the woman said. "I'm Mrs. Pyrzk. What'll it be? Fresh fruit, shoelaces, or how about some apricot shoelace salad?"

MRS. PYRZK'S VERY BERRY BLOOTINBERRY

Mrs. Pyrzk looked at Horace, held out a hand, and gave him a poke with her finger. "What's the matter with you? You're almost invisible. Haven't you been eating enough?" she asked.

The woman's finger jabbed Horace in the lung, making it hard for him to breathe. He backed away a step. "I'm the Cupcaked Crusader. I'm using my superpowers and am going to save the town from the shag carpet creature."

Mrs. Pyrzk sat back in her seat and let out a howl of laughter. "What are you talking about?"

she asked. "A shag carpet creature? That's crazy talk."

Horace pointed at the shag carpet creature as it wiggled against the outside of the store window. "Haven't you noticed this? The shag creature is why it's dark in here."

Mrs. Pyrzk did a little jig, dancing over to the window. "Oh, wow! I thought the sun went down early yesterday and forgot to come up this morning," she said. She put her hand out to open her window. "That rug looks mighty pretty. Maybe I should take a piece to make a door-mat."

Horace gently took her hand from the window. "No, you can't let it in. It's dangerous and covers the whole town. I need a glass of fresh Blootinberry juice to drink so I can get more special superpowers to defeat it."

The woman danced back behind her counter and picked up a scoop, then danced over to a store shelf. "Well, I have plenty of fresh Blootinberries. I can mix you up a glass. What size do you want? Small, medium, large, or colossally colossal?" She took a scoop of dark orange berries from a bin and dumped them in a bowl. "Would you like it hot or cold?" she asked. "Spicy or sweet? With cream or mayonnaise? How's about I add a pinch of Pyrzkinomin. That's my special spice," she said with a wink.

Horace thought about how much both he and Sugar would need. "I'll take one large, cold, and sweet."

Mrs. Pyrzk took a spoon and began mashing the berries. "Plain? I hate plain," she said. "But I guess the Cupcaked Crusader knows what he needs." She mashed harder, whipping the berries into a chunky, frothy broth. She poured the mix into a plastic cup. The thick juice slowly plopped out of the bowl and filled the cup. The juice looked as if it were lumpy, orange paste.

Mrs. Pyrzk did her little jig to her cash register, set the cup down, pushed a few buttons, and turned a crank. "That'll be three dollars and ninety-seven cents," she said.

Horace fumbled through his cape pockets. All he had was the cupcake. Superheroes didn't usually carry money with them, did they? He leaned on the counter with an elbow. "Uh, hey there, nice lady. I was wondering if I could pay you back later," he said, grinning his biggest grin. "I left my wallet in my other cape."

A stern look crossed Mrs. Pyrzk's face. Her eyes darted back and forth between the Cupcaked Crusader and the cup of juice.

Horace could feel something in his body beginning to change. He looked down and saw that his feet were now on the floor and he wasn't as ghostlike as he used to be. The powers from the first cupcake were beginning to wear off. He had to walk back through the wall before the powers went away and he was stuck inside like everyone else.

He held out his hand. "Please, I promise I'll pay you back. I'm a very good friend of Sugar Splattly. She said she comes here all the time."

The old lady raised her eyelids and slowly held the cup out to the superhero. "Well, okay," she said. "I suppose any friend of Sugar Splattly can be trusted."

Horace took the cup of juice. "And she has a nice cousin named Horace," he said.

Mrs. Pyrzk put a finger to her chin and shook her head. "I don't think so," she said. "I only remember the girl." The old woman smiled. "Sugar's such a sweet girl. She's so polite."

"Well, next time look for her cousin. He's a good guy," Horace said. He walked over to the wall, holding the cup of juice. "Thanks for your help. I'll pay you back soon."

Mrs. Pyrzk nodded. "You better," she said, making a note on a pad of paper. "Three dollars and ninety-seven cents. If you don't pay by tomorrow, I'll send the police after you."

"Uh, okay," Horace said. "'Bye." He stepped back through the wall and out onto the shag-carpeted street of downtown Blootinville, just in time to see his body turn back to being solid again.

Chapter 15

TWO PAIRS OF SPLATTULAS

The shag carpet creature grabbed at the Cupcaked Crusader. Now that he was a normal kid again, the long pieces of carpet could crawl up his leg and hold on to him. Sugar was where he'd left her down the street in front of the beauty salon.

"Run, Horace! You have to get to me before the rug can stop you!" she called.

Horace held the cup of juice and dashed down the rug-covered street. When the shag tried to grab at his feet, he hopped, skipped, and leapt over it as best he could.

But it was no use. Without powers, there was no way he could escape the rug. Thousands of pieces of shag reached up at the same time to grab both of Horace's feet, cementing them to the ground. The shag held his feet and ankles so he couldn't budge from his spot.

And Sugar was still six feet away.

Horace reached into his wing pocket and took out the cupcake. "We have to act fast, before the carpet completely covers me," he told his cousin. He unwrapped the foil and took out the cupcake. "Can you get your arms loose and stretch out a hand out to reach me?"

Sugar shook her head. "No, the carpet won't let me move my arms, and I can't get my mouth down there to eat the caramel away. Save yourself first, then worry about me," she said.

"No superhero gets left behind," Horace said. "Just wait a second." The shag carpet crawled up Horace's legs. He looked at the cupcake in his hand. It was green like a pile of moldy cheese and smelled as if it had been sitting on the bottom of a garbage can for a week. Did this cupcake hold the powers to save all of Blootinville?

He broke the cupcake in half and stuffed a piece in his mouth. It tasted like gooey cheese that had been rolled in dirt. Chunks of the cheese got caught between his teeth and clung to his gums.

He lifted his hand with the second half of the cupcake. "How good are you at catching food in your mouth?" he asked Sugar.

"I don't know," Sugar said. "I usually don't play with my food or get in food fights."

Horace smiled. "Well, I'll try and keep it clean," he told her. "Ready?"

Sugar tilted her head back and opened her mouth as wide as she could. "Ready!"

Horace took aim and tossed the cupcake through the air. It hit his cousin on the nose, bounced to her chin, rolled around the rim of her lips and dropped into her mouth.

"*Swoosh!*" Horace called. "I should be a basketball player."

"Good throw, Cupcaked Crusader!" Sugar

said. She chewed and swallowed the cupcake, making a sour face. "This is revolting!" she said. "I like having superpowers, but couldn't your sister make the cupcakes taste better?"

"Hold on," Horace said. He drank half the cup of Blootinberry juice as Melody had instructed. The juice was sweet and helped get rid of the yucky taste from the cupcake. He stretched out his arm as far as it could reach toward his cousin. "How am I going to get you the juice?" he asked.

Sugar bent over as far as she could, leaning

her tongue out of her mouth. "Just throw it in my face, and I'll catch as much as I can," she said.

"I thought you didn't get in food fights?" Horace asked with a grin.

"Sugar Splattly doesn't, but the Annihilator does!"

"Okay, here it comes," Horace said. He lifted the cup, held it high, and tossed the thick, gloppy juice through the air.

Plop!

It landed all over his cousin's face. Sugar

blinked her eyes. "I think I got most of it in my mouth!" she yelled. She swirled her tongue all over her cheeks and chin and under her nose.

"Good catch, Annihilator!" Horace told her. "Now, we just have to get powers and save the town."

The kids stood in the middle of the road. Nothing happened. No powers came.

The shag carpet crawled up to Horace's waist. If he didn't get powers soon, he'd be completely covered.

"Do you think we were supposed to drink the juice before we ate the cupcake?" Horace asked.

"I don't think so," Sugar said. "Do you think your sister made a mistake with the recipe?"

The shag grew over Horace's chest, wrapping around his neck. The carpet grew back over Sugar's face, covering her mouth. "Mmm-phhm-mmm," Sugar said.

Horace lowered his eyes to see the shag carpet reach for his mouth. He had talked to the carpet before, maybe he could do it again? "Uh, don't be in such a hurry to cover me," he told it. "You're just making me angry. You'll be sorry when—" The carpet clamped his mouth shut and slithered over his cheeks.

Horace shut his eyes, trying his hardest to feel if any powers were coming. Should he have bought the colossally colossal–size juice instead of the large? He felt his body growing warmer and warmer. It was as if he had a fever, but he didn't feel sick. He just felt really, really hot as if he were inside an oven. But instead of being in the oven, he felt like he *was* the oven. His hands were changing, too. His fingers felt as if they had melted together and were getting flatter and harder, as if they were being pressed together.

Were these the superpowers or was this what it felt like when the rug tried to shrink you?

Seconds later, Horace got his answer.

The Big Flip

All at once, the rug fell off Horace's body and dropped to the ground. It lay there in a pile of melted caramel and shag. It didn't even try to reach for him. And instead of having hands, Horace had two sharp metal spatulas attached to his arms. They glowed bright red, as if they'd been heated in a fire.

"Look, we're free!" Sugar said.

Horace saw that what had happened to him had also happened to his cousin. "Our bodies are so hot, it just melted the caramel off us, so the rug couldn't stay attached anymore," he said.

"I bet I know what these are for," she said. She bent down to the carpet and slid her hot spatula hands under the rug, flipping it so she could see the street. "It's easy," she said. "You try it."

Horace slid his spatula hands under the carpet and flipped it off the ground. His cousin was right—it *was* easy. The spatulas melted the caramel, so the shag fell flat and couldn't grow anymore.

The two superheroes knelt side by side. "Okay, Annihilator, let's get this thing going," he said.

"I agree," Sugar said. "Let's roll this rug to the cleaners."

The Cupcaked Crusader and the Annihilator dug their spatulas under the carpet, flipping it away from the ground. Step by step, they flipped more and more of the rug. The carpet had soon become a big, gooey roll of shag and melted caramel.

The superheroes flipped more of the carpet.

The bigger the roll got, the faster it fell, dropping off the sides of buildings, lampposts, and the statue of Mayor Blootin in the town center. Horace and Sugar ran across the ground with their spatulas out, scraping and chasing the carpet away.

People stuck their heads out the windows of stores and buildings.

Madame Chantilly Bellray stood in the doorway of her salon with Mr. Howlly. "The Cupcaked Crusader has saved us!" she said.

"And the Annihilator," Horace shouted. "She's the newest superhero in town!"

"But I only annihilate bad guys," Sugar explained. "I'm nice to good guys!"

"Glad to hear it!" Mr. Howlly said.

People leaned out the windows of their homes.

"Hey, Cupcaked Crusader, can I be a superhero with you sometime?" Sara Willow asked.

Horace stopped and smiled at Sara. "That might be fun," he said.

Sugar tugged at Horace's cape. "Come on, Cupcaked Crusader, we're not done yet."

Horace bowed to Sara. "See you later, miss," he said.

Chef Quaquaqua sat on his doorstep in his bathrobe. Spaghetti and meatballs covered his hair. "Ahhh, it's nice to be outside again!" he said.

Sugar and Horace flipped the shag carpet off Blootinville Elementary, the International Town Dump & Airport, the Tippy-Toe Dance Studio, and the Nip & Tuck Plastic Surgery Center. They flipped it up and over Society Hill, where Auggie and Xax lived.

The twins and the family's blue pet poodle leaned out their bedroom windows and waved to their best friend.

"Good going, Cupcaked Crusader!" Auggie yelled. "Who's that new superhero?"

"I'm the Annihilator!" Sugar said. "I'm very tough and mind my manners."

"Where did you come from?" Auggie asked.

"Sorry, but I'm not allowed to tell," Sugar said.

"Do you want to come over for lunch some-time?" Xax asked.

"I'll have to ask my mom," Sugar said.

Horace pretended he didn't know the twins so his cousin wouldn't find out he'd told Auggie and Xax about the cupcakes. "Uh, it's nice to see you, fellas! Say hello to your father," he said.

"Ruff-ruff," Mitsy barked. "Bow-wow-wow-eeeeee!"

The roll of carpet was over fifty feet high. It sped faster and faster through town. It cruised right up Rumbly Mountain, stopping at the top and balancing on its peak.

The two superheroes stood behind the rug, spatulas poised to finish off the job. "Let's do it!" Horace said to his cousin in a tough-guy voice.

"Say 'please,'" Sugar said.

Horace kept himself from laughing. "*Please*, let's do it," he said.

"I'd be happy to," Sugar replied. "Thank you for asking."

The cousins flipped their hot spatulas under the carpet and sent it rolling down the mountain and toward Celernip Bay. Once it splashed into the water, all of Blootinville would be free of the shag carpet creature.

But one building stood in the carpet's path.

Hotel Stalagmite. The giant rolling rug was heading straight for the hotel and looked as if it was going to smash it to the ground.

"We have to get on the other side of the carpet to stop it," Horace said.

"How can we do that?" Sugar said. "It's rolling too fast!"

The Cupcaked Crusader and the Annihilator chased the carpet, but Sugar was right—it was no use. They couldn't reach it in time. In seconds, it would crash into Hotel Stalagmite, toppling it into Celernip Bay with all the Splattlys and Blattlys.

"No!" Horace called to the rolling rug.

"*Please*, stop," Sugar yelled. "I said 'please,' so you have to!"

The carpet didn't listen. It rolled right up against the hotel and looked as if it would crash it down.

But it didn't.

Instead of smashing the hotel into Celernip Bay, the carpet wrapped around the building and began rolling up the hotel, peeling the shag rug off the sides and windows as it went.

Horace and Sugar stood in the hotel parking lot, watching the rug roll up the tall building, until it sat atop the hotel like a giant shaggy caramel doughnut.

"Come on," Horace told his cousin. "Race you to the top." He jabbed his spatula hands into the sides of the hotel and began climbing.

Sugar took a running start and leapt against the side of the hotel, quickly speeding ahead of her cousin.

All the Splattlys, Blattlys, and hotel workers stuck their heads out the windows.

"The Cupcaked Crusader saved the Blattlys!" Nana Blattly yelled.

"The Cupcaked Crusader saved the Splattlys!" Granny Splattly yelled.

Melody leaned out a window. "And he has a new superhero friend named the Annihilator!" she announced.

Sugar scrambled to the top of the hotel and sat atop the giant rug doughnut. "I'm the winner!" she cheered.

Horace finished his climb and sat next to his cousin. He held his spatula hand in the air. "Thanks for your help," he said. "I couldn't have done it without you."

Sugar clanked her spatula hand against her cousin's. "And I couldn't have done it without you," she said.

"Now all we have to do is get our families back together," Horace said.

"I know how we can do that," Sugar said. She leaned over the edge of the rug and peered down at the Splattly and Blattly grandmothers, uncles, aunts, cousins, and parents. "Okay, everybody, it's time we had a talk," she said. "The Cupcaked

Crusader and I want everyone from both families up here immediately!"

"Up there?" Granny Splattly asked.

"Won't the rug make the Blattly women sneeze?" Mrs. Splattly asked.

"Not anymore," Melody said from her window. "Now that the caramel melted over the shag, it can't shed anymore."

"So snap to it and get up here!" the Annihilator commanded. "And, *please*, bring Rugs with you."

THE SPLATTLY AND BLATTLY MEETING AT THE TOP OF THE HOTEL ON THE WORLD'S ONLY SHAGGY CARAMEL DOUGHNUT

The Splattlys and Blattlys sat on the rug in a giant circle atop Hotel Stalagmite. The sun shone over Blootinville, giving the two families a beautiful view of the town and bay. Rugs sat off to the side in a glass container so he wouldn't make anyone sneeze.

Horace and Sugar's powers had worn off, and their hands were back to normal. The two superheroes strolled around the carpet in their costumes, making sure everyone was paying attention.

The Cupcaked Crusader pointed to his mom and dad. "Remember how happy both families were when Mari and Hinkle got married?" he asked.

The Annihilator nodded. "Remember when Mari and Myrtle were friends? Why can't you be happy like that today?" she asked.

Aunt Myrtle raised her hand. "Because Mari and all the other Blattlys hate rabbits and pets," she said.

"That's right," Granny Splattly said.

Horace's mom raised her hand. "We don't hate rabbits or pets; we're allergic to them, and Cousin Crarpet made the rug pet that made us sneeze!"

"That's right," Nana Blattly said. "It's Cousin Crarpet's fault."

"And I'm sorry I ever created the shag rug creature," a voice called out.

All heads turned to the door at the top of the hotel.

Crarpet Splattly stepped onto the rug. He was tall with bushy hair that looked like a shag carpet. He even wore a shag carpet shirt and pants. "I thought having a shag carpet pet would be a fun way to decorate homes," he said. "I didn't know it would grow to be so big and try to eat the town. And if I'd known that the Blattly women were allergic to the pets, I'd never have told Sugar she could bring Rugs to the reunion."

"But Myrtle knew about the sneezing, and she let Sugar bring Rugs," Mrs. Splattly said.

"That's right," Nana Blattly said.

Aunt Myrtle stood. "I was still angry that Mari made me choose between her and Sniffles when we were kids," she said. "I guess that was silly of me, but I loved my rabbit, and she shouldn't have told me I had to give him away or she wouldn't be my friend anymore."

Mrs. Splattly stood. "I suppose it wasn't fair to make you choose," she said.

The Cupcaked Crusader took his mom's hand. The Annihilator took her mom's hand. "We've had enough trouble making the town safe from this shag rug creature to have to worry about your families fighting," she said.

Horace nodded. "How about both families forgive one another and from now on we keep pets away from family reunions?" he asked.

The two superheroes looked from Mrs. Splattly to Aunt Myrtle. "How about it?" Horace asked.

The two women smiled, reached out, and hugged.

Nana Blattly and Granny Splattly nodded at each other and shook hands.

"It would be a shame for our families not to get along," Granny Splattly said.

"Let's go have a reunion and celebrate," Nana Blattly said. "You can even bring Rugs if you keep him in that cage."

"Thanks for helping our families, Cupcaked Crusader," Dr. Splattly said to his son.

"Thanks for saving the town from the shag rug pet," Cousin Crarpet told Sugar.

"But how should we get this big shaggy rug doughnut off the hotel?" Dr. Splattly asked.

The hotel manager peeked his head out a window. "Get rid of it? Absolutely not!" he said. "I love it! I think it's beautiful!"

"Hooray for the Cupcaked Crusader and the Annihilator for saving the town," everyone cheered.

"And for giving me the only hotel with a shag carpet doughnut on top!" the hotel manager said.

The Splattlys and Blattlys began heading back into the hotel.

"Wait!" Mrs. Splattly said. "Horace is missing!"

"And Sugar!" Aunt Myrtle cried.

Horace and Sugar looked at each other, not sure what to say.

Melody stepped forward. "They're playing in my room," she said. "Horace was too afraid of

heights to come up here, and Sugar said she'd keep him company so he wouldn't have to be alone."

Aunt Myrtle and Mrs. Splattly smiled. "Well, tell them to meet everyone down in the dining room for the celebration," Aunt Myrtle said.

"I will," Melody said.

Both families stepped into the hotel, leaving Horace, Sugar, and Melody standing on the rug atop the hotel. Sugar picked up Rugs and held him in his cage. The three cousins looked around in every direction.

"We make a pretty good team, don't we?" Melody asked.

"I think so," Sugar said. "I didn't even mind when you were bossy so we could save the town. I only didn't like it when you were bossy just because you wanted to be in charge. It's not very polite."

Melody laughed. "You're probably right," she said. "I'll try to only boss Horace around from now on."

"Thank you," Sugar said.

"Yeah, thanks a lot," Horace said with a smirk.

A serious look came over Sugar's face.

"Is something wrong?" Horace asked.

Sugar looked at her cousins. "You know, I kind of liked being the Annihilator. Do you think I'll ever get to be a superhero with you guys again?" she asked.

Horace smiled at Melody. Melody smiled at Horace. The brother and sister put their arms around their cousin.

"Sugar, I think this is the beginning of a beautiful superhero friendship," Horace said.